THE WIZARD THE UGLY AND THE BOOK OF SHAME

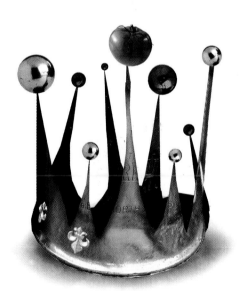

written and illustrated by

PABLO BERNASCONI

BLOOMSBURY
CHILDREN'S
BOOKS

Seventeen thousand, two hundred and nine: that's how many steps there were up to the wizard's castle. It was a long climb to the top, but the journey was worth it, for it was said that the wizard could bring you your innermost wish.

*L*eitmeritz was a responsible wizard who spent all his time studying and mixing potions. He was careful never to let anyone touch his magical things, even his assistant. "Wizardry concerns wizards," he would say, "and that's only me."

Leitmeritz had a secret, something he had been given by his father, who in turn had received it from his father, and so on backward in time to the beginning of memory. Leitmeritz's secret was the Red Book of Spells. It was not a very large book, nor did it look special. Yet condensed on its old pages were the secrets of the world.

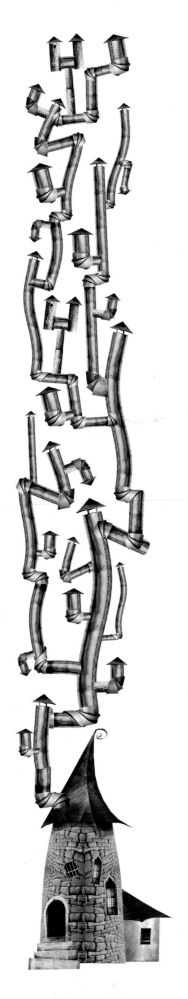

The wizard had an assistant named Chancery. He collected ingredients for the wizard's spells, cleaned the castle and went down to the village for provisions.

Chancery was a sad blue man. And an ugly one. In the village, nobody knew his name. They just said, "There goes the Ugly." Chancery was ashamed of the way he looked.

For years, Leitmeritz had helped all sorts of folk – elves, children, old people, animals, fairies. All of them had come to the wizard with a problem and had left with a solution. All but the Ugly.

"Your shame has nothing to do with magic," Leitmeritz said every time Chancery asked him for help. "It is only the triumph of the mirror!"

But Chancery was still sad.

One morning news arrived that the unicorn, Blanik, was having trouble with a loose horn. After consulting the Red Book of Spells, Leitmeritz hurried off to help Blanik, leaving the castle in Chancery's care.

Later that day the Ugly was sweeping the wizard's chamber, taking great care not to drop or break anything, when he noticed his master's secret Red Book of Spells sitting on a small table. Chancery knew he shouldn't open it, but he just had so many questions . . .

And before he could stop himself, Chancery plunged into the book.

$\mathcal{H}$e saw people and places, and creatures both beautiful and terrible. He saw his hopes in the colours on the white paper and all his fears in the black ink. Each blot was a world.

Chancery's head was dizzy with all the wonders the book contained. But he knew he must concentrate if he was going to fix his problem. And so, at last, Chancery spoke his innermost wish to the book:

"I want to be handsome."

The book suddenly began to tremble and Chancery pulled his hand away. But instead of falling to the floor, the book floated in the air amid lights and strange sounds. All at once, the letters of the book lifted off the pages, then flew in all directions, followed by images, textures and other wonders that Chancery had never seen before.

Then the Red Book of Spells fell down. It was nothing but a heap of blank pages, its contents scattered throughout the wizard's room.

"Leitmeritz will turn me into a plant!" cried Chancery. "Or, even worse, a rock!"

Now not only was Chancery still ugly, but he had also destroyed the wizard's most valuable possession. "I cannot tell him. But how can I repair it?"

There was only one way. The book was empty and it would have to be refilled. Chancery carefully gathered the contents of the book, word by word, letter by letter, and placed them bit by bit on to the blank pages of the Red Book. It took him seven long days. He had only just completed the last page when the wizard knocked at the door of the castle. Leitmeritz had returned!

*D*ays went by. Leitmeritz classified his potions while Chancery assisted him. The wizard had not yet used the book again, but he had no reason to think anything was wrong – until one night when some visitors came to the castle . . .

The first visitor was a toad who began, as all toads do, by asking to be turned back into a prince. "I hate being a toad and I cannot seem to get kissed," he said.

"I will prepare a brew," said Leitmeritz patiently, "that will give you back your royalty." And he went to consult the Red Book of Spells. Some minutes later Leitmeritz returned with a flask of bubbling liquid, which the toad drank immediately.

"I do not feel anything," he began. "Wait . . . Yes, now, yes . . . "

FLOP! The toad was still a toad, but now he was violet with little stars on his body.

"It's never happened like this before," said the wizard. He consulted his book and returned with a new elixir. "Try this."

FLOP! The violet toad became a yellow toad.

Leitmeritz tried again.

FLOP! "Now I am red. Help!"

FLOP! Now he was a graffitied and angry toad. "I must leave before it gets worse. Who will kiss me now?" cried the toad.

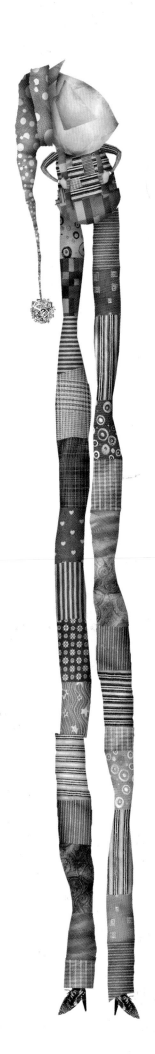

Leitmeritz disappeared into his chamber to review all his formulas. "I do not understand!" he said.

Then a dragon arrived.

Argos was a magnificent old dragon. The villagers feared him, but Leitmeritz considered himself to be Argos's friend.

"My throat aches," complained the dragon. "It must be from all the fire-breathing I do."

"I don't know if I can help you just now," said the wizard, remembering the toad.

"You must help me," insisted the dragon. "It hurts so much. You don't want to annoy me, do you?"

No, Leitmeritz certainly did not want to annoy the dragon. Aided by Chancery, and following the recipe in the Red Book of Spells, he prepared a huge pot of dragon syrup. "Here you are, Argos. Drink it all."

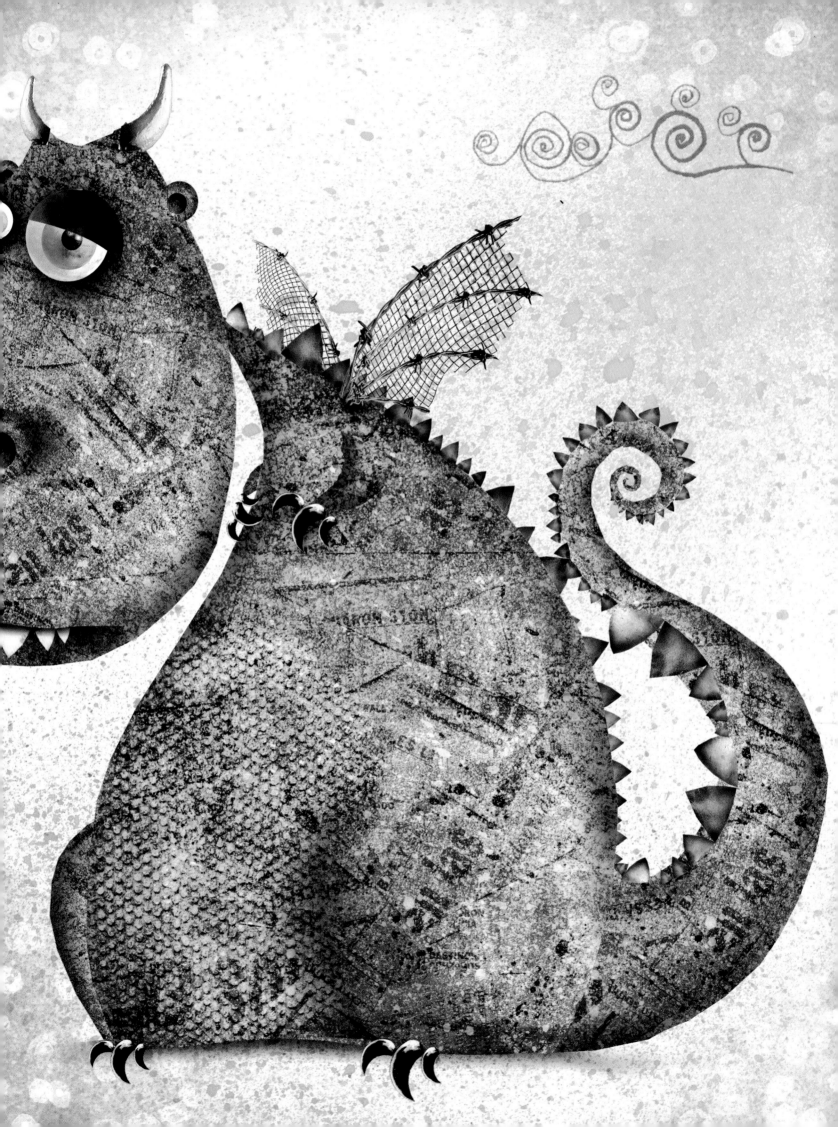

y throat no longer hurts," mumbled Argos, "but now there's a funny taste in my mouth . . . HIC!" A small sky-blue bubble floated out of his enormous mouth. "HIC!" Then another, and another. Chancery watched with wide-open eyes.

"I am breathing soap!" cried the dragon. "Who will be frightened of me now? This is a catastrophe and you are responsible, Leitmeritz. Your magic doesn't work!"

The wizard, horrified, hid himself in the castle, vowing never to use his powers again.

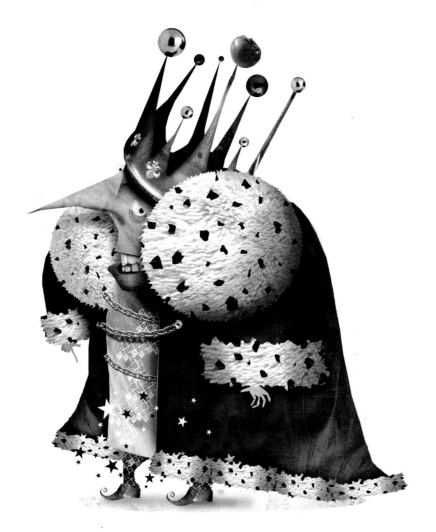

The news spread rapidly throughout the village: Leitmeritz the wizard had closed the gates to the castle and was not receiving anyone. No exceptions. Two long weeks went by without magic. Then Anacreon, the king, set out to see Leitmeritz. He would not take no for an answer.

The king arrived surrounded by counsellors, maidens and knights. He climbed the seventeen thousand, two hundred and nine steps up to the castle. "Open the door, Leitmeritz. Your king is talking to you!"

No answer.

"My word is law, wizard, so open your door or I will batter it down."

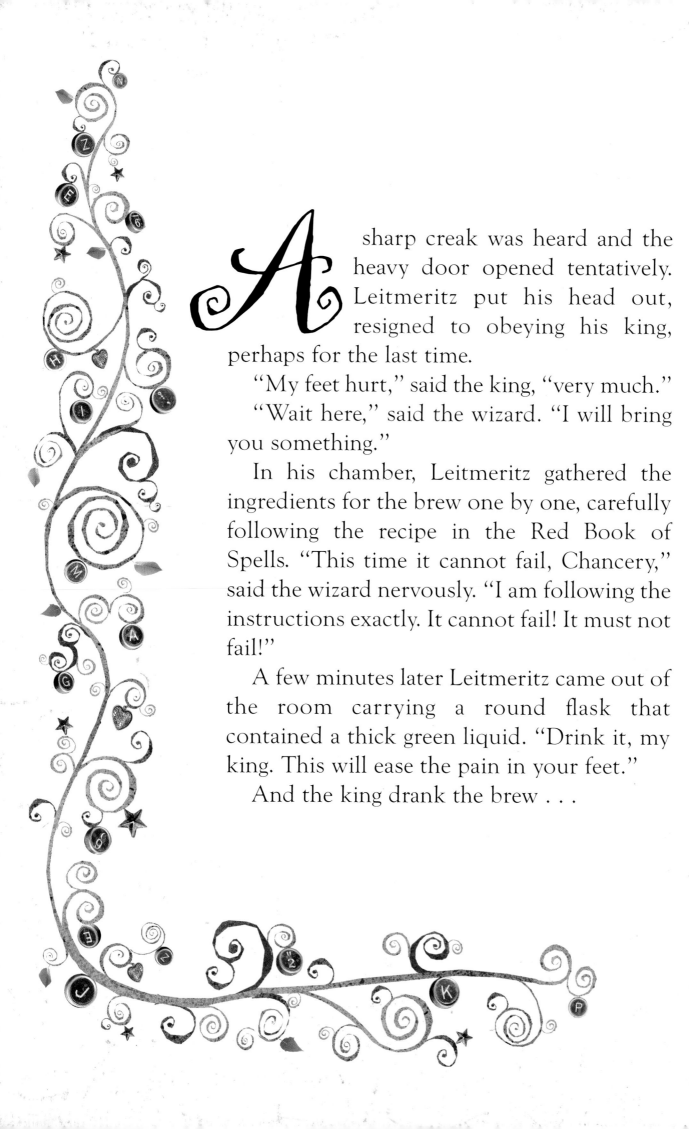

$\mathcal{A}$ sharp creak was heard and the heavy door opened tentatively. Leitmeritz put his head out, resigned to obeying his king, perhaps for the last time.

"My feet hurt," said the king, "very much."

"Wait here," said the wizard. "I will bring you something."

In his chamber, Leitmeritz gathered the ingredients for the brew one by one, carefully following the recipe in the Red Book of Spells. "This time it cannot fail, Chancery," said the wizard nervously. "I am following the instructions exactly. It cannot fail! It must not fail!"

A few minutes later Leitmeritz came out of the room carrying a round flask that contained a thick green liquid. "Drink it, my king. This will ease the pain in your feet."

And the king drank the brew . . .

hat's wrong? What's wrong?" shouted Anacreon. "Why do you look at me like that and why is my head aching now as well? A mirror! Give me a mirror!"

"My king, don't worry – I can solve it," said the wizard, handing him a mirror.

"I have a foot for a head!" roared Anacreon when he saw himself. "What have you done, you fool? How will I gain the respect of my subjects? They will say I think with my feet. Guards! Guards!"

"Stop!" exclaimed Chancery as Leitmeritz struggled with the guards. "Stop! He is not guilty. Release him. It's my fault. It is all my fault!"

"What are you saying, Chancery?" asked Leitmeritz. "I do not understand. What do you mean?"

"I asked the book to make me handsome," sobbed the Ugly. "I'm tired of being the Ugly. I'm sorry, master. Forgive me."

The wizard looked at Chancery. "The Red Book of Spells is very dangerous," he explained. "It was created to be read only by wizards, so if an ordinary person asks the book for anything, it protects itself."

"Find a way to fix it!" cried the king, who watched the scene in anguish with a foot for a head.

"There is one way, but it won't be easy," said the wizard. "Chancery must attain his innermost wish without using any magic."

How could Chancery be seen as handsome when he was the Ugly? His own reflection frightened him – he even disliked his shadow. Yet he had to try.

"To work!" he said. And so Chancery began.

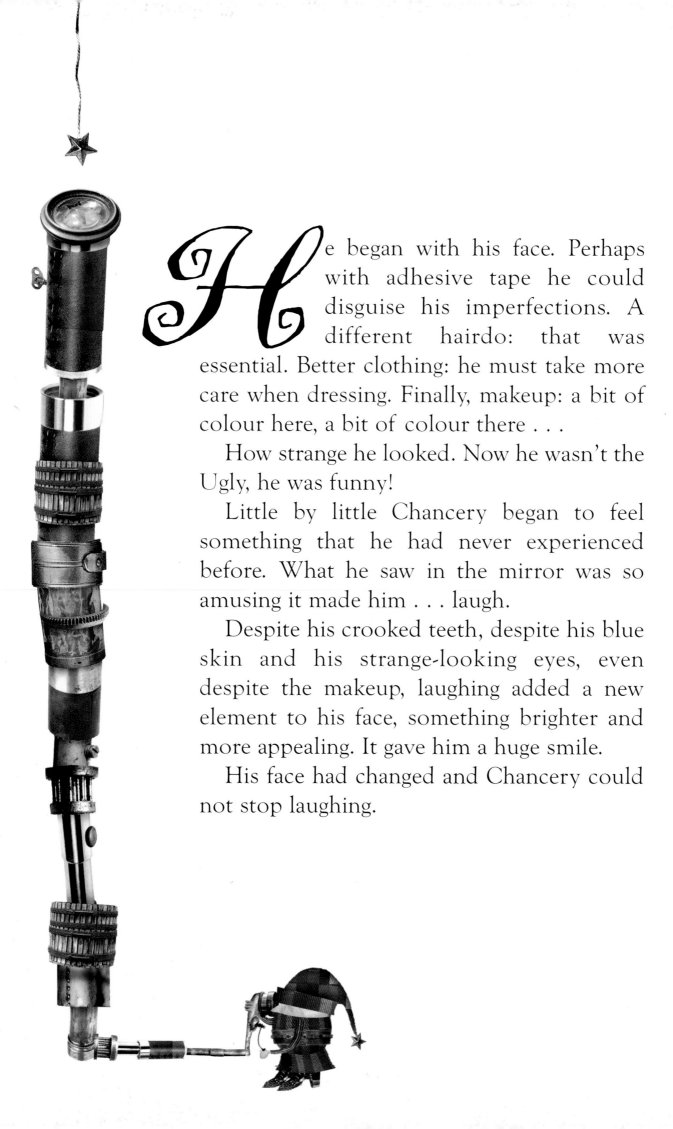

He began with his face. Perhaps with adhesive tape he could disguise his imperfections. A different hairdo: that was essential. Better clothing: he must take more care when dressing. Finally, makeup: a bit of colour here, a bit of colour there . . .

How strange he looked. Now he wasn't the Ugly, he was funny!

Little by little Chancery began to feel something that he had never experienced before. What he saw in the mirror was so amusing it made him . . . laugh.

Despite his crooked teeth, despite his blue skin and his strange-looking eyes, even despite the makeup, laughing added a new element to his face, something brighter and more appealing. It gave him a huge smile.

His face had changed and Chancery could not stop laughing.

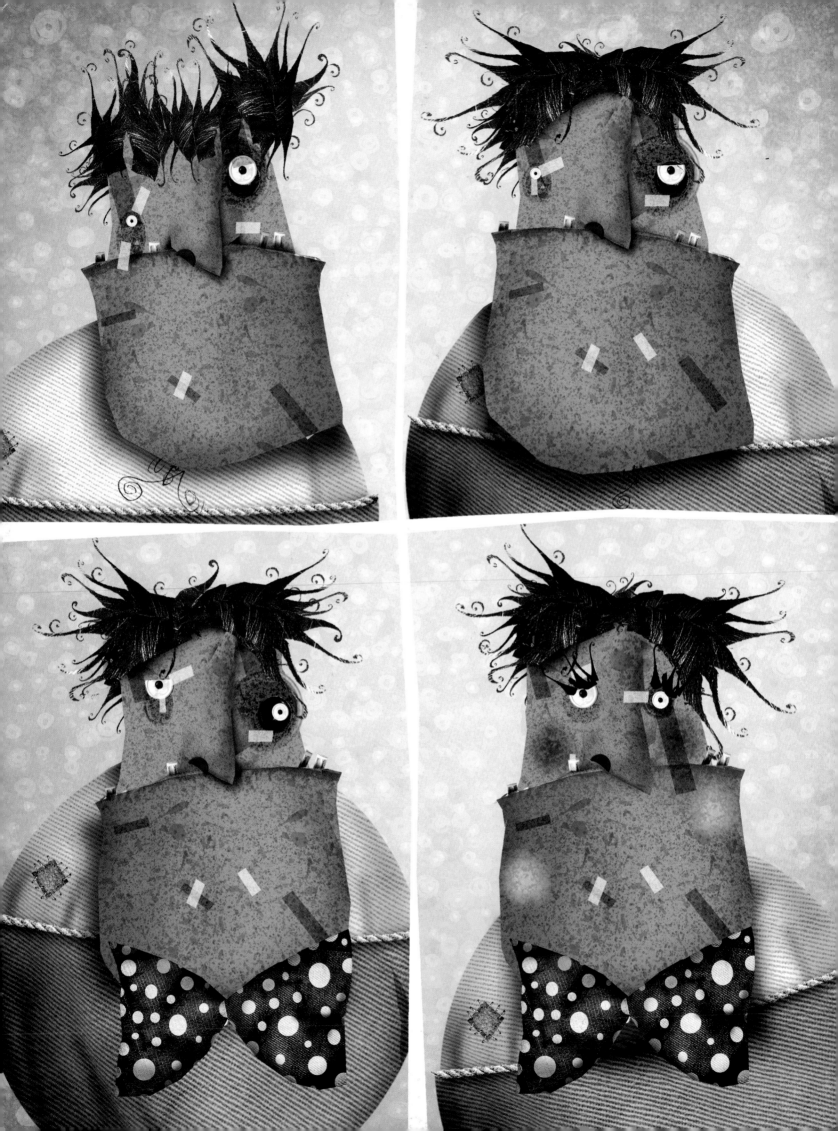

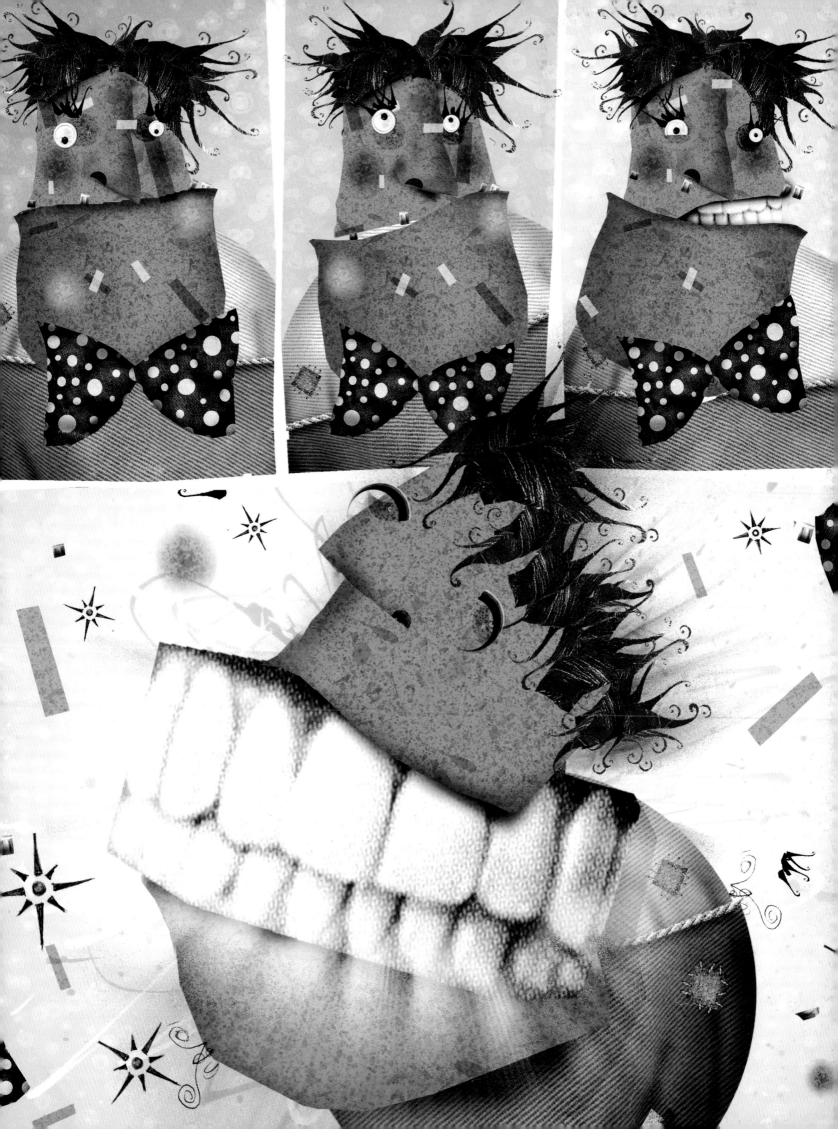

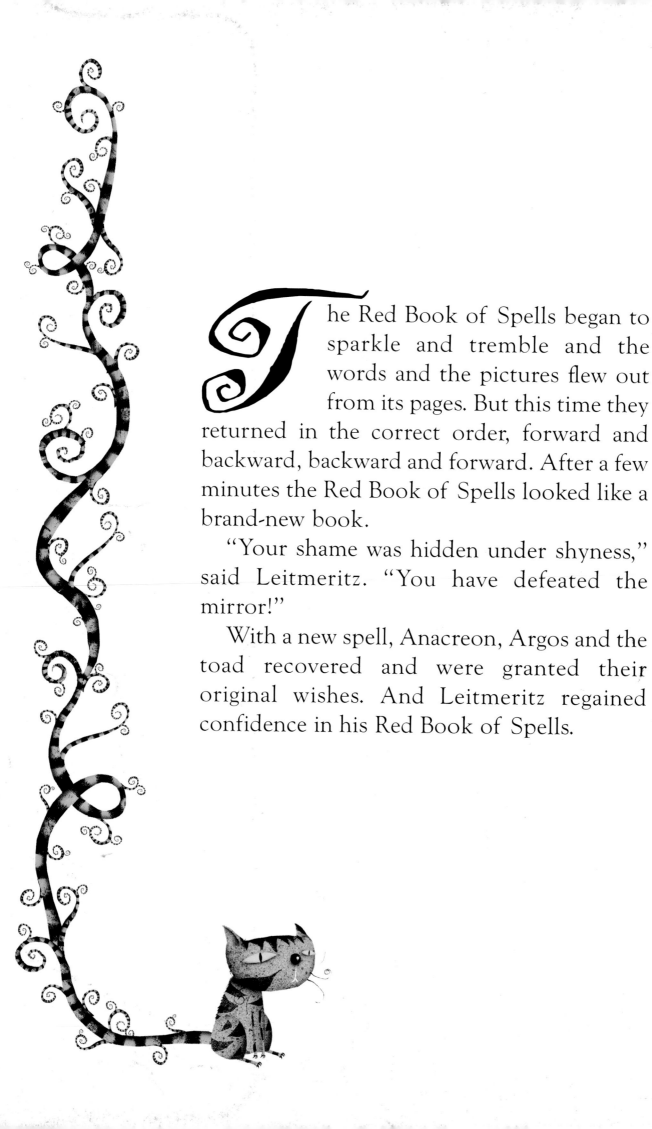

The Red Book of Spells began to sparkle and tremble and the words and the pictures flew out from its pages. But this time they returned in the correct order, forward and backward, backward and forward. After a few minutes the Red Book of Spells looked like a brand-new book.

"Your shame was hidden under shyness," said Leitmeritz. "You have defeated the mirror!"

With a new spell, Anacreon, Argos and the toad recovered and were granted their original wishes. And Leitmeritz regained confidence in his Red Book of Spells.

These days Chancery goes down to the village as often as he can. The villagers don't all know his name, but Chancery no longer cares. In fact, he is proud every time someone points him out and says, "There goes the blue man with the big smile."